Books by Matt Christopher

Sports Stories

THE LUCKY BASEBALL BAT
BASEBALL PALS
BASKETBALL SPARKPLUG
TWO STRIKES ON JOHNNY
LITTLE LEFTY
TOUCHDOWN FOR TOMMY
LONG STRETCH AT FIRST BASE
BREAK FOR THE BASKET
TALL MAN IN THE PIVOT
CHALLENGE AT SECOND BASE
CRACKERJACK HALFBACK
BASEBALL FLYHAWK
SINK IT, RUSTY
CATCHER WITH A GLASS ARM
WINGMAN ON ICE
TOO HOT TO HANDLE
THE COUNTERFEIT TACKLE
THE RELUCTANT PITCHER
LONG SHOT FOR PAUL
MIRACLE AT THE PLATE
THE TEAM THAT COULDN'T LOSE
THE YEAR MOM WON THE
   PENNANT

THE BASKET COUNTS
HARD DRIVE TO SHORT
CATCH THAT PASS!
SHORTSTOP FROM TOKYO
LUCKY SEVEN
JOHNNY LONG LEGS
LOOK WHO'S PLAYING FIRST BASE
TOUGH TO TACKLE
THE KID WHO ONLY HIT HOMERS
FACE-OFF
MYSTERY COACH
ICE MAGIC
NO ARM IN LEFT FIELD
JINX GLOVE
FRONT COURT HEX
THE TEAM THAT STOPPED
   MOVING
GLUE FINGERS

Animal Stories

DESPERATE SEARCH
STRANDED

THE TEAM
THAT STOPPED
MOVING

THE TEAM THAT STOPPED MOVING

by Matt Christopher

Illustrated by Byron Goto

Little, Brown and Company
Boston   *Toronto*

FIRST EDITION

T 03/75

Library of Congress Cataloging in Publication Data

Christopher, Matthew F
  The team that stopped moving.

  [1. Baseball — Fiction. 2. Witches — Fiction]
I. Goto, Bryon, ill. II. Title.
PZ27.C458Tg   [Fic]   74–26911
ISBN 0–316–13940–8 lib. bdg.

Published simultaneously in Canada
by Little, Brown & Company (Canada) Limited

PRINTED IN THE UNITED STATES OF AMERICA

To Sharon, Steve,
Eric, and Jason

THE TEAM
THAT STOPPED
MOVING

1

HIS FINGERS played a nervous tattoo on the receiver as Dick Farrar asked himself for the umpteenth time *Should I or shouldn't I? Why can't I make up my mind?*

Quickly he snapped up the receiver as if this time speedy action would solve his problem. But again he struggled with his thoughts and had to put it back down.

"Man! That's the second time you picked up that telephone and changed your mind," a voice said, startling him. "What's eating you?"

Dick turned and met the elfish grin of his younger sister, Cindy. "I need two more players to make up a baseball team, and the

league starts in two weeks, that's what," he said, somewhat bitterly. "The only guys I know of who aren't on a team yet are Art Walker and Stan Parker. Stan is good, but I heard he and his coach had a fight last year so he's sitting out this year. Maybe he'll play for us, but you know how Stan and I get along."

"Yeah. Like cats and dogs," said Cindy. "Why don't you call up Art and someone else besides Stan?" she suggested.

"Oh, sure. Haven't you seen those two? They're like Siamese twins. One doesn't go anywhere without the other."

Cindy shrugged. "In that case you'll either have to put up with 'em or forget about having a team."

Dick's lips pressed into a straight, firm line. "Not me," he snapped. "I'm not going to give up *that* easy. I'm going to start up a new team and build it up into the winningest one in the league. That's my resolution and I'm not going to back down — even if it means having that bigmouth Stan Parker on my team."

His sister laughed. "How come you're so sure he'll want to play with you?"

"I'll bet on it," he said. He picked up the receiver for the third time, and this time went through with it. He dialed, got Art, and explained what he wanted to do.

"Have you asked Stan?" Art asked when he was finished.

Dick shot his sister a didn't-I-tell-you-so? look. "No, I haven't," he answered.

"Well, ask him first, then call me back. Okay?"

Dick glared at the receiver, felt like plunging it down hard to burst Art's eardrum, but controlled himself.

"Okay. I'll give Stan a ring," he said, anger mounting like a volcano inside him. He called Stan, and it ended up just as he thought it would. Stan said that he'd play if

6

Art did. He also wanted to choose his own position — shortstop — which, to keep the peace, Dick also agreed to.

"Well, you're all set," said Cindy, after he told her the outcome of his phone calls. "Now all you need is a coach and a sponsor."

"I've already got them," said Dick. "Steve Banks, a former semipro ballplayer, is our coach. I told him that I wanted to form a new team to enter in the league and would he coach it if I did. He said sure. The Cool Acres Restaurant will sponsor us. They'll get us our uniforms, caps and balls."

"Well!" said Cindy, brushing back a strand of loose hair that had fallen over her face. "Guess you've been busy! What are you calling the team? I suppose you've already thought of that, too?"

"Of course. I'm calling it the Tigers."

"Tigers? Why so original?"

Dick glared at her. "Because with so many other teams already in the league, we had little to choose from. That's why, smarty!"

At the Tigers' first practice, Coach Banks let the boys choose their own positions, although most of them didn't care where they played. They were pleased enough just to be playing.

For two hours every day before the league started, the Tigers were at one of the two baseball fields in town, practicing diligently under Coach Banks' direction in order to be a strong contender in the baseball league. Dick fretted after the first few days, however. Beyond a doubt Stan Parker was the best athlete on the team. His catches at shortstop and his throws to first base were those of a guy who had played a lot of baseball. And Stan had. He had four brothers, all of whom had played baseball with him since he was eight years old. None of the other boys were within miles of his ability.

The question was: Would Stan stay on the team if he realized that he was a far better player than the other guys?

When Coach Banks said that he had scheduled a practice game with the Panthers, who had finished second in the league last year, Dick shuddered to think of what might happen.

"We'll lose twenty to nothing," he said.

He was almost right.

On the day of the game the Tigers' roster was as follows:

> Mark Patten — *second base*
> Ben Cushing — *third base*
> Stan Parker — *shortstop*
> Andy Michaels — *left field*
> Dick Farrar — *first base*
> Eddie Zimmer — *catcher*
> Jim Tanner — *center field*
> Tony Berio — *right field*
> Art Walker — *pitcher*

The subs were Mike Withey, outfield; Clyde McPherson, infield; and Pat Hammer, pitcher.

The Tigers had first raps. Tiny Phil Sandsted pitched for the Panthers. All he did was throw balloonlike pitches over the plate, or somewhere near it. And all the Tigers did was hit them directly at an infielder or an outfielder, as if that was Phil's intention (which it was). They were out in rapid order — one, two, three.

Art's pitches were so well controlled that it seemed he was throwing the ball through a tube. Just the same, the Panthers enjoyed a hard-hitting first inning, scoring four runs, and repeated the assault in the second inning, scoring six runs. In the third they scored two, and in the fourth, three. It was a regular merry-go-round.

"I guess they're getting tired of running around the bases," Dick said after catching a pop fly behind first base for the third out that ended the fourth inning.

"I think we should give up," Stan remarked as he plunked himself down on the bench beside Dick. "All we're doing is making clowns of ourselves."

"Oh, come on. Give up without a fight?" Dick tried hard not to raise his voice. "Is that what you want, Stan?"

"It's not what I want," Stan blurted. "But I don't like making a fool clown out of myself, either."

"Then you shouldn't have joined . . ." Dick stopped short, realizing how stupid a remark *that* was. "I'm sorry, Stan. I didn't mean that."

"I *hope* you didn't," Stan said, his eyes snapping. "Because if you did . . ."

"Hey, cut it out," Ben Cushing broke in. "We'll never have a team if we start fighting among ourselves."

"Right," said Eddie Zimmer in that soft, almost inaudible voice of his.

"Well! Look who woke up!" Stan leaned halfway off the bench and pinned his eyes on the small but strong-armed catcher. "I thought you did nothing but catch and throw the ball, Eddie!"

Eddie's face turned crimson.

Dick bristled. Darn Stan. He knew as well as anybody what a shy, sensitive kid Eddie was. Why did he have to embarrass him in front of all the guys with that remark?

"Lay off him, Stan," said Dick. "He's doing just as well as anybody else on the team."

A chuckle rippled from Stan as he slid back on the seat. "Never before have I heard of a catcher who didn't open up his trap once in a while," he said, loud enough for the entire bench to hear.

"That's enough, Stan," piped up Coach Banks. "Eddie's doing just fine. Grab a bat, Dick. You're second man up."

Dick gave the little catcher a friendly tap on the knee, then got off the bench and selected his favorite bat, one with a taped handle. He heard the crowd yell as Andy Michaels, at the plate, knocked a pitch out to deep left. The yell died almost instantly as the fielder made a one-handed catch.

"Come on! Let's get up on the scoreboard!" Art shouted.

Dick stepped to the plate and waited for Phil's first pitch.

The score was Panthers 15, Tigers 0.

2

THE PITCH floated in like a lazy balloon.

"Ball one!" shouted the ump.

The next sliced the inside corner of the plate, but Dick let it go by. The third pitch was the real teaser. He swung at it and drilled it over the pitcher's head. The ball sailed out to center field in a hard, shallow drive, and Dick sped to second base for a clean double.

Eddie, up next, lashed a streaking grounder to second. The second baseman fumbled the ball, and Eddie was safe at first and Dick at third.

"Nice going, Eddie!" Dick yelled across the diamond at him.

Eddie, smiling, waved a "thank you" to him.

Jim Tanner fouled the first pitch, then missed the next two for a strikeout. The Tigers groaned as they saw their chances for getting up on the scoreboard going down the drain.

Right fielder Tony Berio came to the rescue, drilling a sharp grounder through short that scored Dick. Eddie raced around to third, but perished there as Art flied out to left. Nevertheless, a small roar and a thunder of feet in the stands went up as the Tigers broke the barrier. The score was now 15–1.

"We're a bunch of dingalings," Dick heard Stan say to Art as the pair started out to their positions. "And I'm the chief dingaling."

"You think it's too late to quit?" Art said.

Stan shrugged. "I don't know."

"Well, let's."

Dick listened carefully, finding himself heading toward second base instead of first in order to catch Stan's reply.

"No, we'll wait," Stan said. "Coach Banks wouldn't like us to quit right off the bat. Of course, Dick wouldn't either, but who cares what he . . ."

Dick glanced over at Stan just as Stan glanced over at him. Stan's face pinked, and his lips tightened as he looked away.

"Wouldn't you know it?" he muttered half under his breath.

The Panthers picked up two more runs, one from a line drive at Dick that was too hot for him to handle. 17–1.

In the top of the sixth, the Tigers' last chance to redeem themselves, Mark Patten uncorked a triple to left center field, and scored on Ben's single. That brought another happy roar from the faithful Tiger fans who apparently felt that their green team, with some luck, might still run up seventeen runs to beat the Panthers.

Stan's cannonball shot over second kept up their faith. The blow advanced Ben to third. Andy's hot drive to short resulted in a double play — second to first. Two outs. One man left on.

"Wake up, Dick," Stan said as the plate umpire looked toward the dugout for the next batter to appear. "You're up."

Dick shook himself loose from the dream-like state into which the Tigers' scoring spree had put him. He picked up his bat and hurried to the plate, his heart pounding, his face hot and sweaty. The first pitch drifted in so slowly that Dick could see the colored threads.

"Strike!" boomed the ump.

"C'mon, Dick!" Stan cried. "Don't just stand there! Swing!"

Phil Sandsted delivered the next pitch almost in the same spot. This time Dick

17

swung. *Smack!* A hard blow to left field! The ball soared like an eagle as Dick dropped the bat and raced for first base. He touched the bag and headed for second. But a groan sprang from the fans — the familiar, disappointing sound that meant only one thing, an out. He looked out to left field and saw the fielder come running in, the ball nestled in the pocket of his glove.

The game was over. The Tigers lost it, 17–2.

"Oh, so what?" Eddie said as he, Dick, and two other guys helped Coach Banks pile the equipment into a couple of canvas bags. "We had a lot of fun, anyway. I know I did."

"Trouble is, Eddie, everybody doesn't feel as you and I do," Dick said sadly.

"Don't worry about it," Coach Banks said. "We were hitting pretty good in that last inning. That ought to be a good sign. It was only a practice game, anyway."

Dick's parents and Cindy walked home

with Dick. The elfish smile on Cindy's face warned Dick that she was just bubbling over with funny things to say to him. *Funny to her,* he thought, *but not to me.* She was only waiting for their parents to stop talking a minute. They were both trying to make Dick feel better about the lopsided loss.

Her chance didn't come until they arrived home. "You guys would have looked better in clown outfits," she said, grinning mischievously. "With your noses painted barnyard red."

"Why, you snail!" Dick snarled, and looked around for something to throw at her. When he saw that he was near her tropical fish tank, he lifted the front cover, dipped his hand into the water, and lifted out a wiggling red swordtail.

"Oh, no! Please put it back! Pleeeease!" Cindy cried frantically. "I take it all back! Just please . . . !"

His anger subsiding, Dick dropped the

19

fish back into the tank, closed the cover and tromped into the kitchen to dry his hand.

His mother looked at him curiously. "What happened, Dick?"

"Sometimes that sister of mine is just too much," Dick answered stiffly.

Mrs. Farrar put a comforting arm around his shoulders and smiled. "Oh, don't let her get under your skin. Sisters are like that. They like to kid their brothers. Deep down inside they're for you all the way."

"Then why doesn't that 'deep down inside' come up once in a while?" he said, his anger practically burned out now.

She laughed. "Don't worry. It will."

A half hour later Cindy was hitting Dick grounders and pop flies in the backyard. It had taken him a while to consent to her offer, but when he realized that she was really serious about it he yielded.

Eddie, who lived next door, came over with a fielder's glove and joined them.

"You'll have to get a catcher's mitt," Dick advised him.

Eddie shrugged. "If my brother hadn't left me this I wouldn't have *any* glove."

Five minutes later Eddie's mother, barely taller than he, stepped out onto the back porch and called to him, "Eddie! I told you that I don't want you to be playing baseball! You'll injure your fingers and that'll be the end of your piano playing!"

"Oh, Mom!" Eddie cried, more embarrassed than disappointed. "I'm wearing a glove!"

"Don't argue with me," his mother replied sternly. Even though she was small — probably weighing less than a hundred pounds — her voice had power. "Come inside. I've got a job for you."

"Job? What job?"

"Never mind. Come in."

"Oh, all right. See you later," he said to Dick and Cindy as he crossed over to his yard and went into the house.

"Man, I feel sorry for him," Cindy said softly. "He's such a nice kid, but you can count the number of friends he has on two fingers."

"And he's nuts about baseball," Dick added. "I hope his mother doesn't insist that he quit. I don't know what we'll do without him."

He was to find out at their first league game against the Foxes. Eddie didn't show up.

3

COACH BANKS had Clyde McPherson, the infield sub, catch in Eddie's place.

The Tigers had first raps. Right off Mark drew a walk. Ben walked, too, and it looked as if the Tigers were off to a good start.

Stan banged out a long, shallow drive over short for a double, scoring the two runners. Then, as if Jack Munson, the Foxes' red-headed pitcher, had jinxed the ball with some magic, he struck out Andy. Then Dick lined a sharp drive right back at Jimmy, who spun on his heels and whipped the ball to second to double off Stan before he could tag up.

Stan kicked the second base sack so hard

that dust puffed off it. "Rotten luck!" he grumbled.

Pat Hammer, the Tigers' alternate pitcher, was able to put the ball right over the plate — and right in the path of Fox bats. The first Fox batter drove a hot grounder down to third that sizzled through Ben's legs to the outfield. The second Fox batter popped a high fly to first that Dick fumbled and missed. The third Fox then slammed a rabbit-hopping grounder to second base, which Mark fielded and whipped to home in an effort to get the runner from third. The throw wasn't bad, but the ball glanced off the edge of Clyde's mitt, rolled to the back-stop screen, and the run scored.

Dick waited for a slow dribbler to come to him, caught it, then raced the hitter to first base and lost.

"Charge those, Dick!" Coach Banks yelled at him.

A Fox struck out, but two more runs

scored before the next two outs were made. Tigers 2, Foxes 3.

Clyde led off in the top of the second inning.

"We know he can't catch," Stan remarked dismally. "Let's see if he can hit."

Clyde blasted a single over second base.

"Well, how about that? He can!" Stan cried, standing up and applauding.

Both Jim and Tony got out, bringing up Pat. Pat took a three-two count, then laced a line drive over second base for a neat double, scoring Clyde. Mark flied out, and that was it for the half-inning.

A Fox doubled on a sharp drive just inside the third base line. The second hitter socked a pop fly high over Clyde's head. Clyde, circling round and round under the ball until he was nowhere near it, missed it by a mile. Then the hitter slammed out a long home run, scoring the runner on second.

Another double followed and next, a

batter hit a dribbler just in front of the plate and Clyde pounced on it like a cat on a mouse. He picked it up and hurled it to first. The throw was wild, and the sixth run scored.

Dick didn't know how they finally got the Foxes out, but they did. When the Tigers trotted in to the dugout, there was Eddie — quiet, shy, peace-loving Eddie — waiting for them, wearing his uniform and cap.

"Eddie!" Dick cried. "Am I glad to see you! What happened, anyway?"

"Mom and Dad had a talk," Eddie said as everyone listened wide-eyed. "Dad won."

"Am I glad!" Clyde exclaimed, throwing his arms around Eddie. "I think that if I were to keep on catching I would be scalped after the game!"

"Well — clipped, anyway," Dick said, smiling. "But nobody's done well, so you didn't have to worry." He saw a chilled look come over Stan's face and corrected himself.

"I'm sorry. I guess that the only guy doing real well is Stan."

The Tigers failed to hit safely in the top of the third inning, which didn't surprise anybody. The Foxes returned to bat, this time uncorking five clean hits and collecting four runs. Tigers 3, Foxes 10.

As each half-inning ended, the Tigers seemed more dispirited than ever. Now and then they hit and scored, but the Foxes, as if they were endowed with some magic formula, were able to do so more often. When the game ended, the Tigers were literally buried, 23–5. Tempers flared after the game.

"I thought that getting up a team would help make friends, not break them up," Dick said to Coach Banks as they collected the balls and bats.

"Well, most of the guys are new at this," he explained. "Each is hurt because he thinks the other guys are down on him for missing a grounder, or a fly, or for not hitting. I'm trying to teach them that we're here to play for the fun of it. No matter what some big leaguers say, my feeling is that winning *isn't* everything. Of course we *want* to win. We do the best we can to win. But somebody's got to lose, too. Must the loser dig a hole into the ground and bury himself?"

He laughed. "I sound like a soapbox lecturer. Take off. I'll see all of you at the next game."

"I like him," Eddie said as he and Dick headed for home behind their parents. "He understands."

"Right, he does," Dick said.

"I hope we don't break up," Eddie said sadly. "Baseball is a lot of fun, and it's good exercise. Better than piano playing! I like it especially because, well . . ." He shrugged, as if unable to find the right words to express himself.

"Because we can all get together once in a while," Dick said. "It's like a party."

"Right!" Eddie said.

That night Eddie came over and the boys played chess. Dick won. It was too late to play another game so they listened to records and talked.

When Eddie left, Cindy said to Dick, "You know that you're the only guy I know who pays any attention to him?"

"Anything wrong with that?"

"No. I think it's super. But why don't the other guys have anything to do with him? I could understand it if he's a creep, but he isn't."

"I guess it's his personality," replied Dick. "He's a real shy kid. You know that he never raises his hand in school when the teacher asks a question? Yet he's one of the smartest brains there?"

"He's wrapped up in a shell," Cindy said.

"Maybe playing baseball will get him out of it."

"Not unless the guys cooperate," Dick replied somberly.

Thursday, June 21, was a day of sunshine and ninety-degree heat. Most of the crowd that attended the Bears-Tigers game sat in the shade of the trees behind the left-field foul line. Only a few braved the scorching sun by sitting in the stands.

The Tigers took the field first. Eddie was behind the plate and Art was on the mound. Dick wished that Eddie would do some yelling to help perk up the team, but he knew that no one could force Eddie to do anything.

The game started, and the Bears' leadoff hitter pushed a Texas league single over second base. Right fielder Tony Berio fielded the ball and pegged it to first. On the throw in, the hitter raced to second, and Stan

31

yelled at Tony, "To second, Tony! Second! Never behind the runner!"

Stan was right, of course, thought Dick as he tossed the ball to Art. "Stay in there, Art," he said encouragingly.

Art, rubbing the ball as hard as if he were trying to pull its cover off, faced the second batter, then pitched. Crack! A solid hit to short! Stan caught the ball and whipped it to second as the runner, after making a start for third, turned and dashed back. Mark reached out to tag him, but the runner made it in time.

Then Mark bullet-pegged the ball to first. But there, too, the ball arrived too late to nab the runner.

We're playing like a bunch of beanheads! an inner voice screamed inside of Dick. *Are we going to lose all of our games by such terrible scores as 17–3 or worse?*

Then, with runners on first and second, a Bear clouted a long drive to right center field that drove in both runners. It was a stand-up triple. The Bears were on the move.

"Let's *do* something!" Stan yelled, making a fist of his right hand.

It's going to be a long ball game, Dick thought despairingly.

Art pitched. The ball arced like a rainbow. The batter swung as if to drive it out of the state. *Crack!* A slow, dribbling grounder toward first base! Both Dick and Art charged after it.

Suddenly something happened. Something that Dick had never experienced in all of his thirteen years.

The ball stopped. Art stopped — posed in a running position, looking as if he had frozen solid. Even all sound stopped.

Dick looked around, then thought that he, himself, would freeze, too. Everybody on the field and in the stands was like a statue! Nothing moved!

4

"HI, THERE!" said a voice.

Dick whirled.

Less than five feet away from him stood a man, a man Dick had never seen before. He was in his twenties — or was it thirties? It was hard to tell because of his handlebar moustache and pointed goatee, both the color of a flaming fire. He was wearing a white jersey, baseball pants, and baseball shoes. On his baseball cap, set jauntily on his head, was the word "Champ."

"I'm Jack Wanda," he said, flashing a broad smile.

Dick's mouth had popped open, but nothing could come out of it.

Jack Wanda laughed and stroked his moustache. "I know just how you feel, kid," he said. "Every boy I meet for the first time reacts the same way. And it's natural!" He paused and crossed his hairy red arms over his chest. "Let me tell you about myself. I'm kind of a male witch," he went on, a glint of devilish pride flashing in his ice blue eyes. "My specialty is helping teams get started that need help — baseball, football, hockey — you name it. And, believe me, you guys need help. Now — are you ready?"

Dick gulped. "For what?" he managed to blurt out.

"For a lesson in baseball, kid!" Jack snapped as if Dick should have known.

"What about these guys? These people?" Dick swung an arm around at his teammates and the fans, all of whom had not moved from their frozen positions. "Will they always stay like that? Like statues?"

Jack Wanda laughed loudly. "Oh, I'm

sorry I didn't explain that!" he said. "Actually, kid, when you and I are finished with this lesson, everything will go on as if nothing had happened. I've stopped time, you see."

Dick stared, wide-eyed. "You mean all — all over the world?"

"Oh, no. Just yours. At this moment you are my subject, therefore *this* time applies only to you. And me, of course. Now, let's get back to the ball game. Are you ready?"

"Ready," said Dick, still unable to believe that this crazy phenomenon was actually happening.

"Good. You know what would happen if both you and Art go after that grounder, don't you? No one will cover first, and the hitter will get on base safely."

"But — what about Mark?"

"Mark? Well, look at him. He's playing too far back to get to first base before the hitter does. What you should do, Dick, is run back, cover first, and let Art handle the grounder. Get it?"

"Got it," said Dick.

Jack Wanda flashed a smile that seemed to make his moustache and beard more radiant than ever. "Good! See you later, kid. And good luck."

In the next instant he was gone — just like that — and Dick found himself chasing the grounder that the batter had hit toward first. From his right side, Art was chasing after the grounder, too. It was quite likely that a collision would occur unless one of them stopped.

Dick stopped. It wasn't the thought of a possible collision, though, that made him decide. It was the instruction from someone who had appeared to him for a split second — some strange, moustached, bearded character wearing baseball clothes and a cap with "Champ" on it.

Sliding to a halt, Dick spun and dashed back to first base. "Get it, Art!" he yelled.

Art fielded the grounder and snapped it to first. The throw beat the runner by a step.

"Out!" yelled the ump.

The runner on third started for home, then changed his mind as Dick made a motion to throw there.

One out, a runner on third, and the next Bear came to bat. Art fed him a neat pitch over the heart of the plate. *Crack!* A sharp blow to deep center field! The ball hit the tip of Jim Tanner's glove and bounced out to the wide-open field for a home run, much to the enthusiasm of the Bears' fans and the dismay of the Tigers'.

The next Bear popped out to Art, and a ground ball to second base ended the half-inning.

"That's four to nothing," Stan grumbled as he dropped onto the bench. "Looks like it's going to be another circus."

· Eddie socked Dick lightly on the knee. "Nice play at first base, Dick. You, too, Art."

"Right. That was a good play," Coach Banks said. "Darn good thing you changed your mind at the last second, Dick, or no one would have been covering first. You probably avoided a collision, too."

Dick smiled. The strange experience he had just had seemed like a dream. It had to be a dream. Time just didn't stop and everybody didn't freeze like statues. But, a dream like that when you're in the act of playing baseball? It was crazy! — what *was* that man's name? Jack Wonder? No, it was *Wanda*. Dick smiled again.

No one got even close to getting a hit that half-inning. And only Stan managed to get on base, thanks to an error by the second baseman. Sadly, nobody drove him in.

The Tigers held the Bears, and vice versa, for the next two innings. In the fourth, Dick and Art were involved in a play that was almost a repetition of the one that had happened in the first inning. Dick charged after the ball for a moment, then, remembering what had happened in his "dream," raced back to first, getting the hitter out by two steps. That was one play he knew he would always remember to do right.

The Bears picked up two runs in the fifth to go into a 6–0 lead, and it looked as though the Tigers were falling to their third defeat, counting the practice game.

Something happened in the bottom of the fifth, though, that gave Dick hopes that the picture would change. Stan led off with a single, advanced to second on Andy's scratch hit to short, and Dick stepped to the plate.

Ray Coombs, the Bears' dark-haired, left-handed pitcher, looked nervously at the runners on base, tugged at his cap, and pitched. The ball missed the plate by six inches. He threw two more wide pitches, then two directly over the plate.

The next pitch was also in there, and Dick swung. The blast was loud and clear as bat met ball, driving it like a cannon shot to deep right center field. The bases cleared and Dick ran in for his first homer of the season.

The whole Tiger team stood behind the plate waiting for him as he crossed it. They pumped his hands, hugged him, and yelled as if he had won the ball game. Even Stan joined in as if nothing had ever happened between them.

It wasn't till later on that Dick was to think of this happy moment, and wonder if only great plays or home runs would insure friendship between members of a baseball team.

It wasn't right, he thought. *Friendship should exist in spite of anything. If there are arguments, let's hash them out and talk things over. But don't let our baseball team turn into a curse. Don't let our own individual performances decide for us whether we are going to make friends or make enemies.*

The Bears held the Tigers to the three runs, came to bat anxious for revenge, and picked up one run. 7–3.

"Okay, this is our last chance," said Coach Banks as the Tigers came to bat in the bottom of the sixth. "Go get 'em."

Art put on his helmet, picked up a bat, and stepped to the plate.

5

PITCHERS were often placed at the bottom of the batting order because usually they were poor hitters. Coach Banks had a different theory about this. He liked to have a *good* hitter at the bottom of the batting order. If he was a pitcher, the odds were that much better. If he got a hit, the leadoff batter was up next, followed by the power hitters in the lineup.

Art was such a pitcher. He could hit.

He proved it by socking the first pitch over short. Mark struck out. Then Art raced to second on Ben's fly ball to center field, only to turn around and beat it back to first as the center fielder caught the fly.

Stan got up and peppered a line drive over second base, advancing Art to second. Andy doubled to right center, scoring both Art and Stan. Bears 7, Tigers 5.

"Let's get three more!" Stan shouted from the bench. "Come on, Dick! Drive it!"

Dick straightened his helmet, then rubbed the fat end of the bat as he strode to the plate. A lot of weight was on his shoulders now. If he got a hit, depending on how far the ball traveled, Andy might advance to third, or even score. But, if he didn't get a hit, the weight would then shift to Eddie's shoulders. And Eddie had not gotten a hit yet.

Crack! A sharp bullet blow to deep short! Dick dropped his bat and bolted for first. "Safe!" boomed the ump as Dick touched the bag just a fraction of a second before the ball slammed into the pocket of the first baseman's mitt. Andy remained glued to second base.

"Well, I can see the headlines already," Stan said as Eddie stepped to the plate. " 'Tigers drop third in a row. Can anybody help the poor Tigers?' "

Crack! Eddie lambasted the first pitch out — far out — to deep left center field for an indisputable home run!

Screams and cheers such as never had been heard before for the Tigers rang out from the win-thirsty Tiger fans and players as Eddie circled the bases.

The Tigers had copped their first game of the season, 8–7.

"He did it!" Stan yelled, jumping up and down in front of the dugout. "The little stinker did it!"

Dick and Eddie slapped hands. "You came through, ol' buddy!" Dick cried, as happy as if he had clouted the homer himself. "You really came through! How does it feel?"

Eddie, looking as if he wasn't sure what

had happened, replied, "Like I've just hit the first home run in my life!"

"Was it, really?"

"Sure! The Tigers is the first team I ever played on."

Dick poked the little guy on the shoulder. "You're all right, Eddie."

Dick could hardly wait to tell Eddie about the "dream" he had. He couldn't think of what else to call it. It did seem like a dream, yet it had been as real as life. It wasn't until they had arrived home and their parents had gone into the house that Dick found himself alone with Eddie.

"Eddie, you won't believe this, but I had the most fantastic dream!" he said, looking around to make sure no one overheard.

"Dream?" Eddie frowned curiously.

"Well — I'm not so sure it was a dream," Dick confessed. "It happened during the game when a Bears batter hit the ball down to first base and both Art and I went after it.

47

Suddenly, every person on the field and in the stands stopped moving, and this man showed up — a man with a red moustache and goatee and wearing a cap with 'Champ' on it. He said he was Jack Wanda, a male witch, then went on to tell me not to go after the ball, too, but to run back and cover first base. Eddie, it was the most fantastic thing that has ever happened to me in my whole life! I-I'm getting goose bumps just thinking about it!"

Eddie's eyes were like huge marbles. "It sounds kind of weird, Dick. But it must have been a dream. What else *could* it have been?"

"I don't know. But it — it seemed so *real*."

"I think it was your subconscious mind that took over for a while," Eddie surmised, as if he were a minor expert about such things. "That must be the only explanation. Hey, coming over tonight to listen to some of my records?" he asked, changing the subject.

Dick stared at him. Eddie's sudden lack of interest about the dream made him feel as if all the air had been let out of him. "Country music?" he asked numbly.

"Of course." As if "what else is there?"

Dick shrugged. "I don't know. I might for a while."

"I really wish you'd come over. Dad bought me a new record Saturday. Please, Dick? I'd like the company."

Dick thought about it a minute. Eddie had two brothers, but both were older than he, and sometimes hardly gave him the time of day.

"Okay, I'll come over," he promised. "About seven-thirty okay?"

"Okay! Thanks, Dick!" Eddie's face lit up like a beacon as he scrambled up the steps and into the house.

Dick considered mentioning his dream to Cindy or to his mother and father. But, at the last minute, he decided not to. Maybe Eddie was right. Maybe it was really his subconscious mind that had taken over for a minute. Wasn't *that* like a dream, though?

It was too deep for him. He might as well forget about it.

He went over to Eddie's house at seven-thirty and listened to his new country record, plus other country music from his record library. The next morning the boys went swimming at the school pool. About a dozen kids were there — both boys and girls — including Stan and Art.

Dick, Eddie and Art were sitting on the edge of the pool, watching Stan dive off the high diving board, when Eddie remarked, right out of the blue, "Art, did Dick tell you about the dream he had during our game yesterday?"

50

"Eddie!" Dick exclaimed. "For crying out loud!"

Eddie's eyes went suddenly big and round. "Oops! I'm sorry, Dick! I —" He covered his eyes with his hand, and shook his head pathetically.

It was too late. The cat was out of the bag, and Art's interest was piqued. "What dream?" he asked, curiously.

"It was nothing," Dick said, and began kicking the water, splashing it over his legs.

"*What* dream, Dick?" Art persisted. "Tell me about it."

"You heard him, Art," Eddie said. "It was nothing."

"It must have been something, Eddie, or you wouldn't have mentioned it," Art said.

Dick pursed his lips. "Okay. But it's still nothing. Remember when that ball was hit to you in the first inning? Well, it seemed that time stopped and this guy showed up and told me to go back to my base and let you handle the grounder. So I did, and we got the hitter out. It was just my subconscious, that's all it was," Dick added quickly. "Now, what's so interesting about that?"

Then he pushed himself into the water, swam to the other side of the pool and back, climbed out, and grabbed up his towel.

"If you ask me, that sounds kind of weird," Art said, his forehead wrinkled.

"Of course it does," admitted Dick. "I told you it was just my subconscious."

"You've heard of a person's mind playing funny tricks, haven't you?" Eddie said, as if trying to redeem himself by backing up Dick.

But Art kept staring at Dick. "I sure have," he answered thoughtfully.

"I — I've had enough swimming," Dick said, anxious to make himself scarce. "Coming, Eddie?"

"Yes. I've had enough, too," Eddie said, following Dick to the locker room.

"I'm sorry, Dick," he said again inside the locker room. "I really am. I just wasn't thinking."

"Forget it," said Dick. "Just pretend it never happened. Okay?"

"Okay." But Dick could see that Eddie wouldn't be able to shake off that boo-boo for quite some time. He, himself, was mad clear through, though he tried hard not to show it. *You can bet your boots,* he thought, *that Art will tell Stan about the dream, and Stan will spread it around like measles.*

They dressed in silence.

"Want to play catch later on, Dick?" Eddie asked as they started to leave.

Dick shrugged. "Okay. After lunch."

No matter what, he couldn't hold a grudge against Eddie.

54

6

MONDAY, June 25, turned out to be as gray as Monday's wash. All day long it looked as if it might rain. Then, an hour before game time, the sun began to shoot golden sparks from behind the clouds. By the time the umpire shouted "Batter up!" the sun was shining like the bright, happy face of an eager baseball fan.

The Tigers' opponents, the Panthers, had first raps. Dick had not been at the pool since last Friday and he wondered if Art had told Stan about his dream. Neither boy had mentioned it to him as yet, and he hoped they never would.

Art, on the mound for the Tigers, tossed

a pitch to the first batter that went for a clean single over short. The next batter walked, and Dick shuddered to think that this might be another runaway for the Panthers, who had shellacked the Tigers in the practice game.

Then Stan caught a line drive and doubled the runner off at second before he could get back to tag up. Just like that there were two outs. The next Panther lambasted a long drive to deep center to score a run. A pop fly to Dick ended the top of the first inning.

Mark led off with a walk, but perished on first as the next three batters got out, one on a bouncing ball to first, two on flies to the outfield.

Again the Panthers' bats connected with safe, solid hits. Before the top of the second inning was over, four runners crossed the plate.

"They're hitting 'em where we ain't," Andy said as he came running in.

"We'll have to tell those naughty guys not to do that," Stan remarked, planting himself down on the bench next to Art.

"Better yet, let's hit 'em where *they* ain't," Coach Banks put in.

But only Eddie and Jim were able to garner safe hits, which weren't enough. Little Phil Sandsted, the Panthers' pitcher, was having another easy day of it on the mound.

In the top of the third, the Panthers' lead-off hitter socked the first pitch to right center for a clean two-bagger that put him in scoring position. Dick had visions of another long inning and looked at the sky, hoping that the clouds would gather up again and this time drench the field.

There was no such luck. The sun was shining as brilliantly as ever.

Crack! A smashing drive to first! Dick backed up a few steps as he tried to judge the hop. The ball bounced up into his glove and he bolted to first in a desperate race with the batter. He lost by a step.

"Dick!" Stan yelled. "You should've run forward, not backward!"

Dick ignored him as he looked for the runner on second and saw that the boy had advanced to third. Now there were runners on first and third.

The next hit was a Texas leaguer over first base, scoring a run. There were still two runners on — one on third, the other on second.

Again a Panther batter drove a sizzling hit to Dick, a sod-digging one-bouncer. He caught it, touched first. One out and the runners had held. Then Stan snared a pop fly for out two.

"All right, get the third one!" Coach Banks yelled.

The Tigers did, but not before the Panthers drove in the two runs. Panthers 8, Tigers 0. The bottom of the third went by with still another goose egg decorating the scoreboard for the Tigers.

"Eight to nothing," Stan grumbled as they trotted out to the field. "The way things are going we'll be trailing sixteen to nothing by the end of the game."

"Well, that's better than twenty to nothing," Art said.

"Oh, come on, guys," Dick said resentfully. "It'll be thirty to nothing if we don't stop squabbling."

The Panther leadoff hitter belted Art's first delivery a half a mile into the sky, almost directly over home plate. "I've got it!" Eddie yelled, holding his mitt over his head as he waited for the ball. It came down, struck the edge of the mitt, and bounced off, almost clonking him on the head.

"Ohhhhh!" the Tigers' fans groaned.

The Panther then clouted a base hit. Even from first base Dick could see the embarrassed look on Eddie's face.

"Shake it off, Eddie!" he yelled. "You'll get the next one!"

Another foul ball was hit directly over home plate. This time Eddie didn't call for it, although he circled around underneath it as he had done before when the first foul ball was hit above him. Again he held his mitt as he had the first time, and Dick held his breath. *He'll miss it again!* the frightening thought screamed through his mind.

Then, suddenly, Eddie shifted the position of his glove from above his head to down in front of him, pocket facing up. Plop! The ball dropped into it and stuck!

Quickly he grabbed the ball and whipped it to first. The runner, standing about five feet off the base as if expecting Eddie to drop this pop fly, too, now sprang back in

an effort to beat Eddie's lightning throw. He didn't.

"Out!" yelled the base umpire.

A roar exploded from the Tigers' fans. "Beautiful play, Eddie! Just beautiful!" they cried, enthusiastically.

A hopping grounder to third, which Ben scooped up and shot to first, ended the top of the fourth inning.

Dick ran in and hugged Eddie, noticing a sparkle of pride in the boy's eyes, a bubbling of real inner happiness on his face. "It was a beautiful catch, Eddie," Dick exclaimed. "It really was."

"Dick, I —" Eddie paused. His eyes were suddenly as wide as bottle caps.

"What, Eddie?" Dick asked, frowning.

Eddie glanced around, then shrugged. "I'll tell you later," he said.

Andy was first man up in the bottom of the fourth. He doubled on the two-two pitch. Then Dick smashed a grass-cutting single through second, scoring Andy, and the Tigers had their feet off the ground, at least.

Eddie won a free pass to first on four straight balls. Then Jim's shotgun single over third scored Dick and advanced Eddie to second. Tony hit four fouls to the backstop screen, then popped out to the pitcher. Up came Art and blasted Phil's first pitch for a long triple, scoring both Eddie and Jim.

The Tigers' fans went wild, and there wasn't a boy sitting down on the Tigers' bench. They were all standing in front of it, cheering their throats dry.

Clyde McPherson, pinch-hitting for Mark, drove Art in with a single, then got out trying to stretch it into a two-bagger. Then Ben flied out to end the fat, five-run inning.

The Panthers came back, though, tougher than ever. The leadoff hitter smashed a line drive down to Stan that made a crazy hop and bounced over his shoulder to the outfield. Jim fielded the ball and pegged it to Clyde at second. The next hit was a fly to Jim, which he missed, letting the runner on first advance to second.

The Panthers' heavy hitter came to bat then, and poled a thunderous drive over Andy's head for a home run. That was it for the Panthers that inning, but it was plenty. They were leading 11–5 going into the bottom of the fifth inning.

As Dick trotted off the infield Eddie met him, grabbed his arm, and led him to the side of the dugout. "Dick," he whispered excitedly, "I've just got to tell you this!"

"Tell me what?" Dick asked, frowning.

"I — I had a dream, too! Remember that second foul ball? The one I caught?"

Dick stared at him. "Yes."

"Well, while it was coming down, it suddenly stopped! *Everything* stopped, and this . . . this guy appeared! Jack somebody."

64

"Jack Wanda?" Dick's eyes grew wide as he stared at Eddie.

"Yes! Jack Wanda! He told me to change the position of my glove. He said that I held it up wrong the first time, and to hold it down in front of me. He even took my glove and showed me how to do it! That was how come I caught the ball! Otherwise I might have missed that one, too!"

Suddenly a shadow crossed in front of them.

"What are you two guys whispering about?" Stan asked, chuckling. "Did one of you have another wild dream?"

7

STAN LED OFF in the bottom of the fifth inning.

"Come on, Stan! Knock it out of the lot!" Art shouted.

Crack! A streaking shot over second base! Stan dropped his bat and raced to first. He started for second, but dashed back as the center fielder whipped in the ball.

Andy came up and cracked out a hit between left and center fields that went for two bases, scoring Stan.

Dick, still thinking about Eddie's dream, stepped nervously to the plate.

"Strike!" cried the ump as Dick took a vicious swing at Phil's first pitch, and missed.

Again Phil pitched, and again Dick swung — and missed. "Strike two!" boomed the ump.

Dick stepped out of the box, scooped up a handful of dust, and rubbed it over his perspiring hands. He wiped off the excess, took a deep breath, and looked out over the field. Andy was on second. The Panthers were all crouched over, hands on knees, waiting, daring him to drive the ball through them.

I've got to knock Andy in, Dick told himself. *We've got to win this game to give the team the confidence it needs to stay together.*

He stepped back into the box, raised his bat, and watched Phil make his next delivery. It was outside.

"Ball!" said the ump.

The next pitch came down the pipe and Dick swung. *Crack!* A bullet drive over Phil's head! Dick bolted to first, crossed the bag, and bounded on to second.

"Go! Go!" the first base coach kept yelling.

Dick crossed second and headed for third. Suddenly he pulled up short. Andy was still on third base! Brushing dust off his legs!

"Get back! Back!" the third base coach shouted at Dick.

Bewildered, Dick turned and started to return to second base, when something hard struck him on the arm.

"Out!" shouted the base umpire.

Dick stared at the Panther who had tagged him out, then again at Andy standing on third base.

"What happened, Andy?" Dick asked.

"I fell," Andy said. "I'm sorry, Dick."

Dick ran off the field, embarrassed at his own foolish mistake. Accidents such as Andy's happened occasionally. But Dick knew there was no excuse for him to run almost up to third base and not see that the base was occupied.

"I kept yelling at you, Dick!" the third base coach shouted at him. "Wasn't my fault you weren't paying attention. What were you thinking about? That dream?"

It wasn't until then that Dick realized that the coach at third was Stan. His face turned a brilliant red as he ran all the way to the dugout without looking up once.

"It's all right, Dick," Coach Banks said comfortingly. "We're not pros. Don't let it get you down."

Eddie flied out to short for the second out.

"Keep us alive, Jim!" Stan yelled through his cupped hands.

Jim did, with help from Phil Sandsted. He got a walk. With runners on third and first, and two outs, Tony cracked a rainbow drive over second base, scoring both Andy and Jim. Jim just made it, beating the throw from the Panthers' second baseman by half a step. The Tiger fans roared as their favorites inched across their eighth run.

Art's fly to left field was caught, ending the three-run inning. Panthers 11, Tigers 8.

"I heard Stan," Eddie said to Dick as they left the dugout. "He's getting more obnoxious every day."

"What can we do?" said Dick. "He's still our best player. And sometimes I feel as if I'm our worst," he added glumly.

"Well, you're not," said Eddie. "In my opinion, you're our best."

Dick's heart warmed. "You're a pal, Eddie."

Eddie smiled. "So are you, Dick," he said sincerely. "Just the same, win or lose, I'm having a lot of fun."

"I know. You're really opening up, Eddie. You've changed."

"Thanks to you," said Eddie.

"You mean to baseball," said Dick.

The top of the sixth inning started with the Panthers' leadoff hitter smashing a drive out to left field. Andy ran back a dozen steps and pulled it in. Two hits in succession put the Panthers in scoring position, and Dick saw the Tigers' hopes of catching up, and possibly beating the Panthers, going down the drain.

Then a smashing drive streaked directly at him. He caught the ball, touched first. Two outs! He pegged the ball to second, and Stan tagged the runner going to the bag. Three outs! Just like that!

"Nice going, guys," Coach Banks said, smiling from ear to ear as the Tigers trotted in for the final ups. "Now let's pile up a few more runs."

Clyde, the first batter, walked.

"Get a hit, Ben!" Dick shouted. "Keep it going!"

Ben hit, all right, but he was thrown out. The game looked, indeed, as if it were going to turn into another loss for the Tigers.

Then Stan cracked a sizzling liner through the hole between third and short for a single.

Andy beat out a scratch single, his second hit of the game, and the bases were loaded.

Up came Dick. He looked at the scoreboard. The Panthers were leading, 11–8. He could win the game!

His heart pounded as he thumped the fat end of the bat against the plate, then got ready for the pitch.

Crack! A scorching blow over second! Clyde scored, but a quick retrieve by the Panthers' right fielder held Stan at third.

"Keep it going, Eddie!" Dick yelled anxiously from first base.

Eddie took a deep breath as he stepped into the batter's box, exhaled it, and waited for the pitch. The first three floated by for a count of two balls and one strike. Then he swung, blasting a long, solid blow to deep left center field! Stan raced in, Andy and Dick trailing, and that was it. The Tigers had come from behind to win their second game, 12–11.

Eddie was almost crushed by his teammates as they swarmed around him, picked him up, and carried him off the field.

"Now I know what a big league baseball player feels like when he socks in the winning run in a crucial game!" He laughed as he and Dick walked home together.

"And ours wasn't even crucial!" said Dick.

The Tigers' next game was late Wednesday afternoon with the Wolves. Both Dick and Eddie spent most of the day with their parents at the circus that had come to town. The boys went to the baseball field afterward, expecting to see both teams already there and the fans filling up the bleachers.

Instead, there were no teams, no fans. The place was empty.

8

A HORN beeped behind them. They looked around and Dick recognized Coach Steve Banks' brown station wagon. With the coach was his wife, a blond woman Dick had met a few times.

"Get in!" the coach called. "The game's at the park!"

The boys stared at each other, then ran to the station wagon and climbed in. A loose tail pipe rattled as the car took off up the street, the exhaust belching smoke.

"I tried to call you a couple of times today," the coach explained. "Where were you?"

"At the circus," Dick answered.

"That's what I thought. Well, both Jim Conley, the Wolves' coach, and I decided to play the game at Beach Park," Coach Banks went on. "Fortunately, the umpires liked the idea, too. Everybody's bringing a dish to pass for a picnic afterward, and Grace and I have brought enough for you two. Sound okay?"

"Sounds great!" Eddie exclaimed happily.

Beach Park was alongside Swift River, an appropriate name for the fast-flowing river. It was wide and shallow, a paradise for fishermen and an adventure for canoeists. The sight of the river made Dick's pulse tingle.

"Can we go canoeing after the picnic, Coach?" he asked excitedly.

"Well, I suppose so. If you're experienced, that is." The coach's reflection in the rear-view mirror cracked a smile at him.

"Oh, I'm experienced!" he replied elatedly. "I've canoed dozens of times!"

75

The baseball field was far enough away from the river so that even an exceptionally long drive wouldn't be able to roll all the way to it. The picnic grounds were in the hilly woods beyond.

Both teams took batting and infield practice. Then finally the umpires got the game under way. The Tigers had first raps, and right off Mark uncorked a hit that went for two bases. Ben popped out to short and Stan belted a single, scoring Mark. Both Andy and Dick flied out, and the Wolves came to bat.

Pat Hammer, on the mound for the Tigers, got the first two Wolves out on four pitches. The third Wolf slammed a hard grounder down to third which Ben fumbled, scrambled for, caught, and then whipped to first base. The ball sailed high over Dick's head and the Wolf dashed on to second. A sharp line drive directly at Stan ended the first inning.

Eddie, leading off in the top of the second, cracked a shallow drive over second to start a scoring spree that went for four runs before the Wolves could stop the run-hungry Tigers. He flashed a warm smile at Dick as he pulled on his face mask.

"Guess we're rolling today, Dick," he said.

"It's about time, isn't it?" a voice answered from behind Dick. He turned to see Stan's blue eyes pinned on him.

Dick met them with a challenge. "You can't expect us to win every game, Stan," he said defiantly. "Anyway, we have a lot of fun, don't we?"

"Fun? What fun can you get out of playing if you don't win?"

"*I* get a lot of fun out of it, win or lose," Eddie said.

"So do I," Dick said. "And I bet that the other guys do, too."

Stan's eyes flitted from Dick to Eddie and back to Dick like Ping-Pong balls. "You make

78

a pair," he quipped. "Make sure that when you're in those woods you keep out of the sight of squirrels."

Dick glared at his back as Stan ran out to his spot at short. "Punk," he muttered to himself.

The Wolves scored a run in the bottom of the second to put them on the board. Again the Tigers hit and brought home the mail, this time two runs to make the tally 7–1.

The Wolves threatened again in the bottom of the third and again in the fourth. Finally, in the fifth inning, with the Tigers in the lead 9–1, the Wolves began to make an impression. They started to pound Pat Hammer's pitches all over the lot. Two errors and five hits resulted in six Wolves crossing the plate before an out was made.

With runners on second and third, a ball was hit high behind first base and Dick started to backtrack for it. He kept his eyes glued on the ball, which looked pale gray against the intense blue of the sky. He had a feeling, though, that he would never get under it to catch it.

Suddenly, just as the ball was about thirty feet above him and dropping fast, it stopped. All sound ceased. All movement around him froze.

"Okay, okay. Just relax, kid," said a voice Dick recognized immediately. "You're not holding your mitt right to catch that ball."

Dick stared at the familiar figure of Jack Wanda, the witch, or whatever he had seen in an earlier game.

"Oh, hi, Mr. Wanda!" Dick greeted him nervously. "I was wondering if I'd ever see you again!"

Jack Wanda's smile wasn't exactly pleasant. "Oh, you'll see me again," he said. "But not as often as you might wish. I can't let you depend on me to help you out every time you get into a predicament, you know. You've got to learn to help yourself."

Dick blinked, suddenly apologetic. "Oh, I didn't mean *that*, Mr. Wanda," he said.

"Call me Jack," Jack Wanda said, some pleasantness coming into his smile.

"I didn't mean that — Jack," Dick repeated softly.

"I'm sure you didn't, kid. But I had to tell you that, anyway. I have to tell that to all my protégés. They're not all dependable, you know. Some are as helpless as little children. Thank goodness you're one of the more independent ones. Well, let's get down to business. Start backtracking as if that ball is coming down. Okay?"

Dick did.

"See that?" Jack Wanda pointed out. "You can't possibly run backward fast enough to catch that fly even if you were the world's backward running champion. Now, turn your back to the ball and run."

Dick did.

"There, see that? You're running three

times as fast. One more thing. Keep your eyes on the ball. Get the idea?"

Dick nodded. "Yes."

"Okay. Good luck, kid."

"Jack, wait!" Dick cried.

But Jack Wanda was gone. Vanished. The next thing Dick knew he was under the ball that was dropping from the sky. Remembering Jack Wanda's advice, he turned his back to it and sprinted as fast as he could, all the time looking over his shoulder and watching the sphere get larger and larger as it came nearer. At the last second he turned and caught it.

A roar broke from the stands as he pegged the ball to second base, nabbing the runner who had not rushed back in time to tag up. Two outs.

A ground ball to third ended the Wolves' big-scoring inning.

"What a play you made out there, Dick!" Eddie exclaimed as Dick plopped down on the bench beside him. "You kept two more runners from scoring!"

Dick glanced at Eddie and winked. Eddie's eyes widened, his mouth formed an O, and instantly Dick knew that Eddie understood. Neither said another word.

The Tigers did nothing at the plate. The Wolves did, and went on to win, 10–9.

9

"WELL, we blew that one," Stan said irritably as the boys picked up their picnic baskets from Coach Banks' station wagon and a few other cars belonging to their parents and headed for the picnic grounds.

"We were ahead most of the time," Dick said defensively. "That's something."

The players from both teams piled their food onto tables adjoining each other, and the few parents that attended sat and ate with their sons. Afterward they cleaned up the tables and stuffed the paper dishes and cups into garbage cans. Then most of the boys went hiking in the woods. Those who had brought their swimming trunks changed in the bathhouse and went swimming in a small bay of the river.

Dick wanted desperately to take out a canoe, but didn't enjoy going alone. Although canoes and rowboats were available at the park marina for a small sum, he was willing to pay the full cost.

"Eddie, want to come canoeing with me?" he asked.

Eddie thought about it a bit, then shrugged. "Really, Dick, I'd rather hike in the woods. Guess I'm just an old land-lubber."

Dick smiled faintly, then saw Stan and Art look at each other. Stan would be the last person in the world Dick would invite to go canoeing with him. But, if Stan volunteered —

"Do you know how to paddle a canoe?" Stan asked him.

"Of course, I do," Dick answered.

Stan eyed him a moment. "Okay, we'll go

with you," he said. "Do we have to wear life jackets?"

"Bet your boots you do. They won't let you take out a canoe without them. You really want to go? I'm not saying I'm an expert. I've been out a few times, that's all."

"Young man, I thought you said you've been out a dozen times," Coach Banks broke in.

Dick shrugged, blushing. "Well, it's been about that many," he said.

They started toward the marina. Suddenly Dick stopped dead in his tracks. His allowance! He remembered that he had been at the circus most of the day and had squandered most of it!

Quickly he took a small coin purse out of his pocket, opened it and looked inside. There were barely half a dozen coins! Not enough to buy an ice cream sundae, let alone rent a canoe!

"Well, I guess we won't go canoeing," he said gloomily. "I'm almost broke. I — I'm sorry, guys."

"Just a minute," Coach Banks said. He took a bill from his pocket and handed it to him. "Don't forget the change."

Surprised, pleased, overwhelmed — Dick accepted the money, while an expression of amusement came over the coach's rawboned face.

"Thanks, Coach!" Dick said, smiling brightly.

He rented a boat, promising the marina owner that they would return it within half an hour. Then the boys each strapped on a life jacket.

"The best way to paddle is on your knees," Dick advised them as the boys freed one of the canoes tied up at the dock and pushed it into the water.

Dick knelt in the stern of the canoe, Stan

in the bow, each with a paddle. Art sat on the middle seat. They paddled out into the river, a fresh breeze blowing their hair across their faces.

"Isn't this just great?" Dick cried.

"I love it!" Art exclaimed.

For a moment there was no response from Stan, and Dick wondered why he volunteered to go canoeing if he knew he wouldn't enjoy it.

Finally Stan turned and looked over his shoulder. "Where are we going?"

"Up the river," Dick answered. "Then we can coast back on the current."

They headed up the river, the boat rocking gently as they steered it into the current.

"Dick," Stan said after they had covered about a quarter of a mile, "let's hear about that dream you and Eddie have a thing about."

Dick's hands froze on the paddle. He stared at Stan.

"Oh, it's no dream," he said after a moment's hesitation. "It's real."

Art glanced at him, interest glowing in his eyes. "Hey, tell us about it, man!"

Dick shrugged. "Why not? Really, there wasn't much to it. While we were playing baseball everything all at once stopped. And this guy with a red moustache and red goatee showed up."

"I see," said Stan. "And he waved a magic wand and you caught the ball or whatever."

"Well, he didn't have a magic wand, but he did tell me how to play the ball."

"Man!" Art exclaimed, shaking his head. "You'd win the prize for tall tales, old buddy!"

"Sorry I asked," Stan snorted.

Neither one saw the amused smile that graced Dick's face. *I had a feeling they wouldn't believe me,* he thought.

The trio entered a wide expanse of the river where the current seemed to be barely moving, then passed alongside a tiny island, the edge of which was blanketed white with sea gulls.

"Wouldn't it be fun to camp there?" suggested Art.

They paddled on, passing within twenty feet of the rapids. Presently a growing apprehension took hold of Dick. The rapids were getting bigger and fiercer. As if Art's mind were tuned in to his, Art looked around, his forehead creased with worry. "Don't you think this is getting real rough, Dick?" he asked.

"Right. Let's head back." Dick raised his voice. "Stan! Turn around and face this direction! We'll head back for the marina!"

He watched Stan rise carefully to his feet and turn around, then did likewise. But just as he settled down to kneel again, Art decided to change around, too. As he stood up the boat tilted. Then he let out a terror-

stricken cry as the canoe started to capsize.

A much louder yell followed from both Dick and Stan as all three toppled into the swift, rapid-charged river.

10

THE COLD WATER shocked Dick as he went under. Quickly he bounced to the surface, aided by his life jacket and his own struggling efforts.

He spat out a mouthful of water, pushed his matted hair away from his face, and looked around for Stan and Art. Fright gripped him as he failed to see either of them in the moving mounds of the rapids.

Then he heard a gasp. A second later he saw Stan bouncing in the water some ten feet away. Close by him was Art, his eyes wide and frightened, even though his life jacket was keeping him afloat.

"Stan! Art!" Dick shouted. "Are you all right?"

They stared at him, their hair plastered to their heads. "Yes! Are you?" Stan asked.

"I'm okay!" he answered. He looked for the canoe and saw it heading down the river, bottom-side up.

"What about the canoe?" Stan yelled.

"Let it go!" Dick yelled back. "In these rapids we'd be in worse trouble if we tried to turn it over! Come on! Let's head for shore!"

The strong current carried them down the river as they started to swim toward shore. They gained by inches, and at last were close enough to shore to stand up and wade in the rest of the way.

They stood on the pebble beach shivering. "I'm awfully sorry this happened," Dick apologized. "It's never happened to me before."

"Yeah," Stan said, his lips quivering.

Suddenly they heard the *phut-phut* sound of a motorboat, and looked downriver. A small outboard was speeding toward their overturned canoe. It soon reached the small boat, and one of the two men in it turned it right side up, then lifted it to spill out the water while the other man stood searching the river.

The boys started to wave and shout. For a while it appeared that the man didn't see or hear them. Then, at last, he spotted them and waved.

"He sees us!" Stan cried triumphantly.

The first man took a paddle with him into the canoe and started to row toward shore. The second man then gunned the motor of the outboard and shot upriver toward the boys.

Moments later the trio were hauled out of the water and delivered back to the park, where a reception committee of Tigers, Wolves, coaches, umpires and parents

grabbed and hugged them as if they had just returned from a harrowing experience on the moon.

"Come on," Coach Banks said as he ushered the boys ahead of him toward the picnic grounds. "Get to the bathhouse and out of those wet clothes."

"B-but we haven't g-got any dry ones!" Dick stammered, shivering.

"Three of the boys are going to keep on their trunks and let you borrow their clothes," the coach explained.

Ten minutes later they were showered, dried, and in the clothes lent by their teammates.

"Now tell us what happened," Coach Banks said as they sat around a glowing fire. The sun was setting, filling the sky with soft strokes of lavender and pink. The river looked like a rose garden of dancing lights.

"Well," said Art, "Dick wanted someone to go canoeing with him, so Stan and I went.

Everything was fine until we started to come back. We thought that the water was too rough for us to go on. It was when Dick told us to turn around in the canoe that the boat tipped over."

Dick's heart jumped. "Art! You're making it sound as though it was my fault that the canoe tipped!"

"Whose idea was it to go into the rapids in the first place?" Coach Banks asked.

"Dick's," Stan answered without hesitation.

Dick's face flushed up. He bounced to his feet and glued his eyes on the coach. "Coach Banks," he snapped hotly, "when are we going home?"

The coach looked at Stan and Art, then at Dick. "In a minute," he said.

11

THE TIGERS played the Lions on Monday. It was the first time since the picnic that Dick had seen Coach Banks.

"Here's your change, Coach," he said, handing him the change from the bill the coach had let him borrow last Wednesday. "I'm sorry I didn't think of it before."

The corners of Coach Banks' eyes crinkled as he accepted the money. "Oh — thanks. Can you believe it? I haven't slept a wink worrying about whether I'd ever get that change back?"

Dick laughed.

He played a satisfying game, knocking out two hits that accounted for three runs. He

had made an error on one of Stan's throws, but nothing serious happened because of it. The Tigers won, 13–10.

"I didn't tell you that during our canoe ride Stan and Art asked me about my dream," Dick said to Eddie as they arrived home from the ball game.

Eddie's eyes widened. "What did you tell them?"

"The truth. That time stopped and a red-bearded guy appeared."

"And?" Eddie's mouth was as wide as his eyes.

Dick chuckled. "They didn't believe me. Art said I should win a prize for telling tall tales!"

Eddie laughed. "They asked for it, the stinkers," he said. "But then, at first I didn't believe you either."

On Thursday they were tied with the Foxes, 8–8, when an incident happened in the top of the fourth inning. The Foxes were batting and had a runner on second base. A Fox drilled a fast grounder to Stan at short. Stan fielded it and fired it to first. It was one of Stan's wildest throws, and Dick hoped that by stretching out as far as he could he might catch it. Deep inside, though, he felt certain that he wouldn't.

Then for the third time everything froze — the ball halfway to him, the players in their positions, everything — and Dick found himself staring at Jack Wanda. Jack was standing there with his arms folded over his chest, looking at him with a sour expression on his red-moustached, red-goateed face.

"Look, kid," Jack said. "You've played enough games to know that you would never be able to stretch and catch that wide throw. You know what will happen? The ball will zoom by you, the runner on second will run to third and then score, and you'll boot your-

100

self for not doing the right thing in the first place."

"You mean — I should get off the base?" Dick said, his forehead wrinkled.

"Of course! You want to save a run, don't you?"

Dick bobbed his head. "Yes. Yes, I do."

Jack Wanda smiled brightly. "Of course, you do! Okay, kid. Back to the ball game."

Just like that the world became normal again, and Dick found himself starting to touch the base with his left foot and stretching out for Stan's throw. Instantly, remembering Jack Wanda's instructions, he ran off the bag, caught the wide throw, and watched the runner on second rush back to the base.

There were runners on first and second now. At the end of the half-inning they were still there.

The Foxes pummeled the ball hard in the

101

next two innings, however, and came out on the long end, 14–11.

Dick walked home with Eddie, feeling a lump in his stomach. He told Eddie about seeing Jack Wanda again, and about Jack's advice to him on the play at first base. But even Jack's wizardry didn't seem to be enough to give the Tigers the necessary boost they needed. How long could he, Dick, hold them together if they kept getting drubbed?

Stan wasn't present at the Tigers-Bears game on Monday. Coach Banks said that he had gone on a week's vacation with his parents to California. So Clyde McPherson played shortstop. He made only two errors, which was good, considering that he had eight chances altogether. This game, fortunately, the Tigers won, 9–7.

On Thursday the Tigers won again, beating the Panthers 3–1. It was the tightest game of their season so far, and brightened Dick's hopes of keeping the team together.

Just before the game with the Wolves on Monday, Dick realized that not only Stan was absent, but so were Jim Tanner and Pat Hammer.

"Wasn't Stan supposed to be gone only a week?" he asked Coach Banks, the old worry returning to haunt him.

The coach nodded, frowning. "That's what he told me," he answered. "Maybe they decided to stay longer."

Dick saw Art standing within earshot of them. Suddenly Art turned and headed for the dugout.

"Art, have you heard from Stan?" Dick called to him.

Art paused, then said over his shoulder, "Yes, I heard. He's home."

Dick stared. "Why isn't he here? Do you know?"

"He quit."

"Quit?" The word was like a death knell. "You sure?"

Art nodded. "He figured that if we could win two games without him, we don't need him."

"Hogwash!" Coach Banks snorted. "We need him now more than ever. Jim is out because of a bad cold, and Pat will be gone for two weeks on his vacation. If Stan doesn't play we'll be short a player, and you know what *that* means."

"It means we would lose by forfeit," Dick said. "Hold the game up till I get back, Coach Banks. I'll phone him."

He started off on a run, then stopped. "Oh-oh. I need a dime," he said, looking at the coach like a basset hound begging innocently for a handout.

"What — again?" said the coach, but wasted no time reaching in his pocket and handing Dick a dime.

"Thanks, Coach!" Dick said, and bolted away.

He entered a phone booth just outside of the ball park and dialed Stan's number. After two rings Stan answered. "Hello?"

"Stan! This is Dick! We need you, Stan! We'll lose by forfeit if you don't play!"

A dozen seconds cat-footed by. "How can you lose by forfeit?" Stan asked finally.

"We won't have enough players, that's how!" replied Dick, knowing he sounded desperate and was begging, but he didn't care. "Jim is sick and Pat's on vacation! Please come, won't you, Stan?"

Again there was a dead silence. Then a *click!* as Stan hung up.

12

THE FIELD was empty except for the umpires standing near home plate. The Wolves were waiting at their dugout, the Tigers at theirs. Eddie and Dick kept looking at the entranceway to the park, hoping that Stan would pop around the corner at any moment.

The umpires looked at their wristwatches. Then the one holding a mask turned to Coach Banks.

"We'll have to call it, Steve. Time is about —"

"Wait!" Dick interrupted. "He's coming! Stan's coming!"

Every Tiger jumped to his feet as he looked toward the entranceway of the park. There was Stan, walking in as carefree as you please, wearing his uniform, ball cap and carrying his glove.

"Hurry up, Stan!" Dick shouted. "We're ready to start!"

Stan seemed to think about it a few seconds, then broke into a slow run.

"Okay!" the plate umpire yelled. "Play ball!"

The Wolves had first raps, and began to hit Art's pitches as if they were still having batting practice. Three runs scored before the Tigers were able to stop them.

"Maybe it would've been better if I had stayed home and let the game be forfeited," Stan said gloomily as he trotted in to the dugout.

"Don't say that, Stan," Dick said. "I'd hate to lose a game by forfeit."

"And don't say that you don't want to play because we can win without you," Coach Banks grunted at Stan. "We need you at *every* game."

Stan gazed straight ahead, his cap tilted back on his head, his arms crossed over his chest. He offered no comment, as if this time silence spoke louder than any words he could think of.

What an egotist! Dick wanted to shout at him. *I'd like to knock that bullishness out of your head, buster!*

"Pick up a bat, Stan," the coach's voice broke into his thoughts. "You're up third."

He got up, dragged himself to the pile of bats, and picked one out. Eddie and Dick exchanged a look, then shook their heads.

"I almost wish he didn't show up," Eddie muttered softly.

"I know what you mean," said Dick. "But let's hope he makes up for it."

Mark and Ben were thrown out on grounders. Then Stan, after taking two called strikes, smashed a high fly to center that was caught for the third out.

Dick and Eddie looked at each other and shook their heads.

The Wolves picked up another run in the second inning, and two in the third to lead the Tigers 6–0. Then, in the bottom of the third, the Tigers began to unleash power that Dick didn't know they had. Tony started it with a double over second base, followed by singles off the bats of Art, Mark and Ben. Again Stan failed to hit safely, and went back to the dugout, sulking.

The Tigers ended up by scoring seven runs that inning, a feat that restored their waning confidence. Especially Dick's.

The fourth and fifth innings went by with both teams playing equally good baseball. Then, in the top of the sixth, the field looked like a shower of baseballs as the Wolves' bats again knocked Art's pitches all over the lot, scoring five runs. The Tigers were unable to send home more than two, and the game went to the Wolves, 11–9.

"I *knew* I should've stayed home," Dick overheard Stan say to Art as they started off the field.

"Why?" Art said. "We almost beat them, didn't we?"

"Almost — phooey!" Stan snorted.

Dick caught up with them, Eddie at his heels. "Stan," he said, "thanks for coming. I really appreciate it."

"All I did was keep us from losing by forfeit," Stan said. "I didn't get a single lousy hit."

On Thursday, the Tigers tackled the Lions. This time, batting first, they seemed to be starting off on the right foot. Mark lambasted big Bert Quinn's pitch to left center for a triple and scored on Ben's single to right. Stan uncorked a long fly to center, but the Lions' center fielder made a spectacular catch and Stan returned to the dugout, ignoring the comments — "Tough luck, Stan," and "Nice hit, anyway, Stan" — that the Tiger fans showered at him.

Andy and Clyde kept up the onslaught. Then both Dick and Eddie grounded out to end the half-inning. Three runs had scored.

The Lions managed to get one across the plate during their turn at bat. The second inning turned out better than the first for the Tigers. They tallied four runs to the Lions' one. Again Stan failed to get a hit. Dick did no better.

In the top of the third the Tigers' bats were still unleashing furious power, but it was as if each hit were labeled for a specific fielder. None of the three Lions' fielders — the shortstop, the center fielder, the first baseman — had to move a foot out of his way to catch the ball hit to him.

The Lions' bats rang out as loudly, but produced more satisfying results. Three runs crossed the plate before Stan's long throw from short to first, after he fielded a sizzling grounder, made the third out. Tigers 7, Lions 5.

In the next three innings the Tigers chalked up four more runs. But the Lions garnered seven, squeezing by the Tigers, 12–11. Stan had walked once and gotten one hit. He had also committed two errors, the first game in which he had missed more than one grounder.

"I guess the shoe's on the other foot now," Eddie said to Dick after the game.

Dick frowned. "What do you mean?"

"Well, Stan's the goat now," Eddie explained. "He's gotten only one hit in the last two games and in this game he made two errors. That's a record for him."

"I see what you mean," said Dick, wishing he hadn't asked Eddie for the explanation.

The baseball season had gone past the midway point, and so far all the Tigers had stuck it out. They were up there among the leaders, too, which Dick had never expected.

His getting the team together had accomplished something else, also. It had helped Eddie get out of his shell and make new friends. That alone meant an awful lot to him — and to Eddie.

But what about Stan? Did playing with the Tigers help him make new friends, too? Or did it cause him to make enemies? Dick thought about that for a long time. Stan wasn't one to have many friends, anyway. As a matter of fact, he seemed to be satisfied in having only one real close friend, Art Walker. But Stan wasn't one to make enemies, either, except one which he had probably made within the last week. Himself.

On Tuesday, just before the game against the Foxes, Dick learned that Stan had quit the team for the second time. Stan had informed the coach about it over the phone.

"He says he's a jinx to us," Coach Banks explained. "I tried to plead with him, but it didn't do any good. Fortunately, Jim and Pat are back, so we won't forfeit. But not having Stan will make a big difference."

Dick shook his head, and wondered if he should call up Stan again and try to coax him back.

He decided not to. The game was about to start.

13

THE FOXES batted first and drew first blood. They scored twice in the first inning, and once in the second inning while the Tigers remained literally at a standstill.

A hit had sailed by Mark that Dick thought Mark could have nabbed had he tried harder. Then Ben made a weak attempt in catching a grounder that bounded over third base, and which Andy grabbed up in left field and pegged to second base instead of third, all of which accounted for the Foxes' three unearned runs.

"Come *on!*" Coach Banks exclaimed, glowering at the boys as they sat in the dugout like a covey of nervous birds. "Half of you guys look as if you've been up most of the night watching the late-late show. Snap out of it! Hustle after those balls! What's eating you, anyway?"

No one could tell him. Or wouldn't.

Only Dick and Eddie knocked out hits, both singles, in the bottom half of the second inning. But even those hits were not enough to spark the other Tigers.

In the top of the third the Foxes continued on their way, knocking Pat's pitches all over the lot to the tune of seven runs. Three were on errors by Clyde, whose little finger on his right hand had been injured on the first grounder hit to him. After that he had favored the finger and could neither catch nor throw very well.

When the Tigers came to bat, Dick's thought about calling up Stan rocked back and forth in his mind like a pendulum. One moment he wanted to call him up, the next moment he didn't. He didn't know what to do. Stan might not want to play, anyway. He had refused when the coach had asked him. Why should he change his mind for Dick?

I'll call him, anyway, Dick decided at last. *I've got to try, at least.*

Noticing that Tony, the Tigers' first batter, was still at the plate, Dick took off at a fast run.

He sprinted all the way to the phone booth, dropped in the dime he had come prepared with, dialed Stan's number, and got Stan's mother.

"This is Dick Farrar, Mrs. Parker," Dick said, gasping for breath. "Is Stan there?"

"Just a minute."

Then Stan's voice came on. "Dick," Stan said belligerently, "you shouldn't be calling me. I've told Coach Banks —"

"Stan, please come to the game," Dick interrupted. "We're behind ten to nothing, and the guys don't have the spirit. They all want you to play. You can't let us down, Stan. You've got to —"

"Ten to nothing?" Stan echoed.

"That's right. Ten to nothing."

"But it's too late now, isn't it?"

"It's never too late, Stan. Hurry! I've got to go now. See ya!"

He hung up and raced back to the field.

"What did he say?" Eddie asked.

"He didn't," said Dick.

The Tigers didn't score during that inning either. They returned to the field, moving like windup robots with their springs half run down.

"Hustle!" Coach Banks ordered gruffly. "Hustle out there!"

Then, just as the Foxes' leadoff batter stepped to the plate, Dick saw a familiar figure come into view at the park entrance.

"Here comes Stan, you guys!" he cried, jumping to his feet. "HERE COMES STAN!"

119

The guys leaped and shouted with joy as Stan came running in toward the dugout. Coach Banks pointed at the shortstop position and waved Clyde off the field. Dick caught Eddie's look and winked.

"Play ball!" shouted the ump.

Pat Hammer pitched, and the Foxes' lead-off batter uncorked a drive over second base for a single. Then Pat walked the next batter, and Dick's heart sank. *Will things really be any different now with Stan playing?* he wondered despairingly. *Well, it was still too early to tell.*

Then, *crack!* A smashing grounder right to Dick! He backed up two steps, caught the hop, then rushed to first. The hitter beat him to it.

"Safe!" shouted the ump.

"Oh, Dick!" Stan started to yell something else, but cut himself off short.

"I know," Dick said, angry at himself. "I shouldn't have backed up."

Stan turned and started to kick at the sod when suddenly the players, the umpires, the fans, a dog running across the field — all froze. All, except Dick — and Stan.

And there, standing between them, stood Jack Wanda. A bright smile was on his red-moustached, red-goateed face as he looked at Dick. "Hi, kid," he greeted warmly. "Missed me?"

"Jack! You bet I did!" Dick cried. "We really need you, Jack! Stan, this is Jack Wanda. You know, the guy I was telling you about."

Stan, his foot inches away from the sod he was about to kick, put his foot down and stared at Jack. "I-I can't believe it!" he exclaimed, his face the shade of milk.

Jack chuckled. "Well, kid, seeing is believing, isn't it?" he said musingly.

Stan gulped and nodded.

"I have the most fortunate ability to stop time, Stan," Jack explained. "I'm sort of a

coach, and my job is to help new teams —
baseball, football, volleyball, you name it —
get off to a good start. Frankly, I'm rather
proud of the Tigers. You boys have done
much better than many other teams that
have needed my help. I've only had to help
you a few times, and I think you can make it
on your own now. There is one thing, however, that is badly in need here."

The boys' full attention was riveted on
him.

"That thing is sportsmanship and team-
manship," Jack explained seriously. "Without those two qualities no team could last
very long. You could see it for yourselves.
Since you started to play you became more
like enemies, not friends. You saw what happened today. Half of the boys wanted to
play, half didn't. All because of you two."

A lump rose in Dick's throat as he looked
at Stan and Stan looked at him.

"I was hoping that Coach Banks would

drive this point home to you," Jack said. "Since he neglected to do so, I decided that I should."

"I-I'm glad you did, Mr. Wanda," Stan said humbly. "It's been me. I know. I . . . I have always been too mouthy. Most of the time I just can't help it." He looked at Dick. "I'm sorry, Dick."

Dick smiled. "Aw, forget it," he said.

"Okay," Jack said. "Go back to your positions. Win or lose, play so that your fans will be real proud of you. Promise?"

"We promise!" both boys answered at once.

They returned to their positions. Suddenly Jack was gone, and everything was back to normal again. Dick noticed, too, that Stan had not followed through with his kick. He had spun around and was now smiling pleasantly at him.

"Let's go, gang!" Stan shouted. "Let's get 'em!"

As if the Tigers had drunk some kind of magic potion, they began to play much better than they had before and proceeded to keep the Foxes from scoring. Then, during the bottom of the fourth inning, they began to hit Jack Munson to the tune of eight hits and seven runs. In the fifth inning they garnered three more to tie up the score, 10–10.

"One more run!" Dick shouted as the Tigers came to bat in the bottom of the sixth. "Just one more!"

Stan led off and smashed out a scorching double. Andy flied out to center. Dick, stepping up nervously to the plate, realized that the game could go into an extra inning unless he, or Eddie, got a hit to score Stan.

"Knock me in, Dick!" Stan shouted from second base. "Powder it!"

Dick watched Jack Munson's first pitch breeze by him. "Strike!" cried the ump.

Another pitch rifled in. "Strike two!" bellowed the ump.

"Dick — please!" Stan yelled.

Crack! A long, shallow blow to deep left center field! Thunder rocked the Tigers' bench as Dick dropped his bat and raced around the bases, holding up at third.

It was over. The Tigers won, 11–10.

The boys jumped up and down and hugged each other as if they had won the championship.

"I can't believe it!" Coach Banks exclaimed as he stood among them, beaming proudly. "Stan, your coming to finish up the game with us made all the difference in the world!"

Stan's eyes shone like bright lights. "It wasn't only me, Coach. It was Dick, too. And Jack Wanda."

The Coach frowned. "Jack who?"

Dick laughed. "Jack Wanda!" he cried. "A new friend of ours, Coach! You should meet him sometime! Right, Eddie?"

"Right!"

Coach Banks' eyebrows rose in wonder and amusement. "You guys!" He laughed. "What are you going to think of next?"